This diary belongs to:

Pippa Morgan

TOP
SECRET

Check out my other totally AMAZING diaries!

Pippa Morgan's Diary

Pippa Morgan's Diary
Love and Chicken Nuggets

First published in the UK in 2015 by Scholastic Children's Books
An imprint of Scholastic Ltd
Euston House, 24 Eversholt Street
London, NW1 1DB, UK
Registered office: Westfield Road, Southam, Warwickshire, CV47 0RA
SCHOLASTIC and associated logos are trademarks and/or registered trademarks of
Scholastic Inc.

Text copyright © Hothouse Fiction Limited, 2015
Illustration copyright © Kate Larsen, 2015

The rights of Annie Kelsey and Kate Larsen to be identified as the author
and illustrator of this work have been asserted by them.

ISBN 978 1407 14596 9

Printed and bound by CPI Group (UK) Ltd, Croydon, CR0 4YY
Papers used by Scholastic Children's Books are made from wood grown in
sustainable forests.

1 3 5 7 9 10 8 6 4 2

www.scholastic.co.uk

Thank youuuuuuuuuuuuuuu,
Kate Cary!

Wednesday evening

I have just watched the BEST SHOW EVER!
It's called *Most Spooky* and it's even
better than *CopShop*! I still love *CopShop*,
btw. It's a TV programme about real-
life detectives. Detective Inspector Mike
Hatchett is my hero. But *Most Spooky*
is about ghosts! Not dressing-up-for-
Halloween-in-a-sheet type ghosts but . . .

REAL GHOSTS!

Mike Hatchett only hunts criminals, but on *Most Spooky*, they hunt ghosts.

Ghosts can do all sorts of cool stuff criminals can't, like:

1. Float through walls.

2. Be invisible.

3. Make supernatural noises.

4. Move stuff without even touching it.

I bet criminals wish they were ghosts. Mike Hatchett would never catch them. Ghosts are like criminals with SUPERPOWERS!

(I wonder why ghosts don't rob banks? Or smuggle diamonds? Perhaps they do and we <u>just don't know!</u>)

Anyway. . .

I can't believe I've never watched *Most Spooky* before. It's totally awesome. Mum warned me it might be scary. And it *was* scary, but I LIKE being scared (so long as it's not falling-down-the-stairs/house-on-fire scared).

Most Spooky stars Sally Pippin and Marcus Flaunch. Sally Pippin is an ordinary TV person, but Marcus Flaunch is a REAL ghost hunter. He's super-psychic and he can tell when there's a ghost in a room just by feeling the air! He gets all goosebumpy and keeps rubbing his arms and shivering and looking over his shoulder. Then he says to Sally Pippin something like: "I can tell someone is trying to communicate with me," or, "There has been much sadness in this room." And he suddenly pauses and holds up a finger and says, "Do you feel that?" And Sally Pippin looks all spooked and starts peering around the room (it's usually an old house because more people have died in them) and she'll say, "I feel cold."

Then Marcus Flaunch just nods and says, "That's the Presence" in a really dramatic voice. (A "Presence" is a ghost that you can feel but can't see. I guess it's like when I know Mum's cross and about to tell me off, but *way* spookier.)

Marcus Flaunch has special ghost-detecting equipment. He has a sound recorder to detect ghost noises. And a thing that looks like a mobile phone for detecting ghost energy (ghost energy is a bit like electricity but more tingly). And a thermal camera, which sees hot and cold instead of light and dark.

Three Ways to Detect a Presence

1. The air turns icy cold.

2. You hear strange noises (like moaning or knocking or doors slamming).

3. Ghost energy makes your ghost detector crackle.

In tonight's programme, Marcus and Sally didn't see any actual ghosts, but Marcus could definitely feel something ghostly in the room and his equipment detected lots of cold and noise and ghost electricity.

(Sally Pippin didn't notice *anything* weird apart from feeling cold, but ghost-hunting equipment is probably a lot more sensitive than a TV presenter.)

ANYWAY.

I have decided to become a ghost hunter, just like Marcus Flaunch!

Now is the perfect time because, on Friday, my class is going on a school trip to the Isle of Wight. We're staying all weekend! In a hotel! And we're going to visit Carisbrooke Castle, which must be full of ghosts because it's <u>ancient</u>. All I have to do is pack some equipment so I can detect them.

<u>Packing List for School Trip</u>

- My ghost-hunting journal.

- Sound/video recorder for ghost detecting (I'm borrowing my dad's old phone. It can do both. He said I must only use it for Important Stuff, but ghost hunting is most definitely Important, so I know he won't mind).

- Thermal detector (the thermometer from the medicine cabinet).

- Energy detector for ghost electricity (my fluffy blue jumper. The fluff sparks on my hair when I put it on. If hair makes it spark, I bet *ghost electricity* will start the blue fluff crackling like crazy!).

- Pink pig pyjamas (not really ghost-related, but they're my favourite).

- Sweets (for a midnight feast!). ☺

Catie just texted me! She's really excited too. We're going to be sharing a room in the hotel. Squeeee! It's going to be the greatest sleepover ever because Catie's my best friend in the whole world. (*Rachel* is too, but she moved to Scotland a few months ago and it's hard to do best-friend stuff when there's four hundred miles between us. Rachel and I will ALWAYS be best friends, but having two BFFs is brilliant. I am SO lucky.) I wonder if me and Catie can get a room next to the twins? Julie and Jennifer have been to the

Me

Catie

BFF

Isle of Wight before, but they were so young they don't remember it. I'm going to text them and remind them to bring sweets  for the midnight feast!

Bedtime

I'm snuggled up in bed. I've finished
packing my Isle of Wight bag.
It's at the bottom of my bed,
squashing my feet, feeling as
full as a Christmas stocking
on Christmas Day. I know I'm
not going until Friday, but
if I pack now I'll have time to
remember any stuff I've forgotten.

Mum wouldn't let me take the thermometer
from the medicine cabinet. She said I wasn't
going to get ill and, even if I did, she was
sure one of the teachers would have a first-
aid kit with a thermometer.

ME: But I have to take it for ghost hunting.

MUM: Will you be looking for sick ghosts?

ME: No! I have to check the air temperature.

MUM: Not with my thermometer. You might lose it.

ME: I won't. I promise!

MUM: You promised the same thing when you took the box of plasters to school.

OK. She was right. I lost the plasters. But it was worth it. Me and Catie wanted to

play *Emergency Room* in the playground.
We planned to be doctors like on the TV
show, but we couldn't find anyone who
wanted to be our patients. We thought we
could help when Jason fell over, but he
wanted the dinner lady to put a plaster
on his knee and not us. Then we offered
to operate on Julie and Jennifer but
they didn't want to lie on the playground
while we swapped their kidneys. We tried
to do the operation anyway but it's really
hard to operate on someone while they're
skipping.

Anyway.

Mum said I couldn't have the thermometer. So, after tea, I decided that I'd *practise* feeling cold. I kept putting my hand in the fridge to see what it felt like when the temperature suddenly drops. But Mum  told me to stop opening and closing the fridge door. She said if I kept flapping the door, the light bulb would break.

ME: But it's an important experiment. I need to know what it feels like when a ghost is in the room.

MUM: There's no such thing as ghosts.

ME: How do you know?

MUM: Because I've never seen one.

ME: But you believe in Father Christmas even though you've never seen him. (I knew Mum would *have* to say <u>yes</u> because she always makes me leave out FOUR chocolate cookies and a BIG glass of sherry for him on Christmas Eve.)

MUM: I guess so.

ME: So if Santa exists, why can't ghosts?

MUM: Ghosts aren't the same as Santa.

ME: They're not *exactly* the same because Santa's not scary. But they're both *paranormal.* (Marcus Flaunch says "paranormal" all the time. I think it means the opposite of normal. Like cats that say woof or rain that falls upwards.)

I'm not actually sure if Father Christmas *is* paranormal. But it didn't matter because Mum changed the subject and said it was bedtime. And I guess it was. But both me and Mum knew that saying "It's bedtime" is practically the same as saying "You're absolutely right, Pippa. Ghosts *must* exist."

I'm turning my bedside light off now,
even though I'm way too excited
to sleep.

I can hardly believe it. In less than three
days, I'm going to find a ghost
on the Isle of Wight. And when
Mum sees the proof, she's going
to HAVE to believe me!

Thursday (morning break)

ONE DAY TILL THE ISLE OF WIGHT!

It's raining so hard outside, there are rivers running down the playground. There's a big puddle at the bottom and it's getting bigger. What if the school floods? That would be exciting! We could turn the desks upside down and paddle them around the assembly hall. I could be a lifeguard and help rescue the year threes by letting them climb aboard my desk boat!

Because of the rain, we're staying in the classroom for break. Mr Bacon is at his desk marking our maths homework. I hope that's not my book he's looking at because he's got the same disappointed expression he gets when Jason Matlock can't remember his four times table.

Jason is actually sitting down. He's usually got more energy than a puppy with a sugar rush. Mr Bacon finds it hard to make him sit through lessons. Seeing him sit down during *break* is a miracle! Tom and Darren brought in their DragonQuest cards and they're showing him how to play. Mandy Harrison is playing Bop It with Sophie, the new girl. Well, *Mandy's* playing Bop It while Sophie watches. Every time

Mandy offers her the Bop It, Sophie just shakes her head and looks away.

Sophie Geranium Furnival-Smith is super-shy. (Isn't that the best name *ever*? I'd LOVE to be called Pippa Geranium Furnival-Smith. I'd insist everyone call me Pippa Geranium all the time.) But Sophie Geranium Furnival-Smith doesn't seem to care that she has a fantastic name. She hardly looks at anything except her feet. She's only been here since Monday (I think she moved from somewhere in Cornwall). And she doesn't smile.

She looks like this. ☹

Perhaps *all* Cornish people look like this. ☹

Or perhaps she's a duchess or a princess. That would explain her brilliant name. Maybe she went to a really posh girls' school where there are fluffy carpets on the floor and all the chairs are velvet and they write with ink pens just like people from the olden days. If she did, our school must seem really weird to her. We have lino floor tiles and plastic chairs. *And* we have boys. I wish I could go to a girls' school. I'd be able to walk across the playground without getting hit in the head by flying footballs.

It takes a while to get used

to being hit by flying footballs. Perhaps that's why Sophie looks like this ☹. Me and Catie and the twins keep trying to play with her at break times. We know where all the quiet, football-free places are. But Sophie just hangs around the cloakroom door and, when we ask her to join in, she looks at her feet and blushes.

When I asked her if she was coming on the Isle of Wight trip yesterday, she just shrugged and said, "I guess."

She didn't seem at all excited.

How could she not be excited?

HOW?

Catie's sitting next to me, playing Jenga with Julie and Jennifer. They asked me to play but I've got plans. If I want to become an expert ghost hunter by the weekend, I'm going to need to do some research. I'm going to ask Mr Bacon if I can go to the school library to see if there are any books about ghosts.

Maybe — as well as a ghost book — I can find a book on how to make people happy. If I can, I'm going to borrow it and see if I can find a way to cheer Sophie up.

I asked Mr Bacon if I could go to the library and he said yes. So I raced there

and went straight to the science section,
but there weren't any ghost books. I
did find one in the history section. It's
called *British Myths*. I'm not sure it has
any ghost-hunting tips in it, but when I
flipped through it, I saw lots of pictures
of crumbly houses and chapter titles like
"The Hanging Monks" and "The Headless
Corpse."

In the last chapter there was a picture
of a beautiful lady ghost. I read the story
next to it. Hundreds of years ago, an Evil
Baron tried to force a young woman
to marry him. But she didn't want to
marry him. So she locked herself in a
tower and starved herself to DEATH.
(I could never do that. I like pizza too

much.) Then she haunted the Evil Baron's
castle until he promised to become a
Good Baron and he gave all his peasants
nice houses to live in and swore he'd
never force anyone to marry him again.
And her ghost blessed him with a ghostly
kiss and disappeared and was never seen
again.

I wonder if someone is trying to force
Sophie to marry an Evil Baron. It would
explain why she's so sad.

   No. It can't be that. She's too young to
get married. But perhaps she lives in
a haunted house. After all,
if she's a duchess or a princess,
she probably lives in a castle

and, according to Marcus Flaunch, castles
are ALWAYS haunted.

Or maybe she has a tragic
secret. Like an extra toe
(I must remember to check
when we're getting changed for PE this
afternoon), or she's an orphan, or she has
a wicked stepmother who makes her sleep
in the cellar, or she's a vegetarian. Imagine
never being allowed to eat chicken nuggets!
That would make me sad.

I decided I absolutely HAD to cheer her up.

AN OFFICIAL DECLARATION

I, Pippa Morgan, do hereby declare that it
is my DUTY from this moment forth to
make Sophie happy, for ever and ever, till
death us do part.
Amen.

Pippa Morgan

So, while I was checking out my British
myths book, I asked the librarian what
books make people happy.

The librarian crinkled up her eyes, like

she was thinking really hard. She was quiet for a bit, then she said, "What about a joke book?"

I thought that was a brilliant idea. I followed the librarian to the funny books section and found a book called *The World's Funniest Jokes*.

Once the librarian had scanned it for me, I hid it under my jumper so that Sophie wouldn't see it when I got back to class.

I'm going to spend the rest of the break learning as many of the jokes as I can. Then I'll tell them to Sophie during PE. I am going to make her laugh before the end of the day.

I just know it!

Thursday teatime

(I'm writing around the food
splatters on my ~~diary~~
ghost-hunting journal. I'm in the kitchen
while Mum cooks stir-fry for tea. Mum's
kinda enthusiastic about stir-fry. The wok's
hot enough to melt spoons. The ceiling is
hidden in smoke. Mum's had to silence the
alarm twice. Vegetables are bouncing
around the wok like bunnies on a
trampoline.
Who knew
sweetcorn
could jump so far?
I think there's a bit
in my hair.)

ANYWAY.

My plan to make Sophie smile started
OK. I'd learned FIFTEEN jokes during lunch
break and I managed to
get on Sophie's team for Benchball.

Ms Allen made Sophie the goalie, so I
tried my hardest to score a point
so I could stand next to her on the
bench. Tom scored before me, but I scored
next. So I stood on the bench as close to
Sophie as I could. She was watching the
ball, ready to catch it if it came towards
her. She was frowning so hard! So I tried
my funniest joke first.

ME: *(whispering)* Sophie! What's orange
and sounds like a parrot?

SOPHIE: *(watching the ball)* What?

ME: What's orange and sounds like a parrot?

SOPHIE: *(turning to look at me, surprised)* Why?

Unfortunately, while Sophie was looking at me, a ball came flying towards her. It hit her on the side of the head and bounced back into the other team's half of the court. And they scored.

Uh-oh. I guessed that Sophie wouldn't be feeling very smiley after that, so I decided to save my next joke for maths.

BTW: While we were getting changed after PE, I made an excuse to walk past Sophie while she was changing her sweaty socks. She definitely doesn't have an extra toe, so *that* can't be why she's sad.

When I got back to Catie on the other side of the changing room, I whispered, "No extra toe." (I'd told her all my theories on why Sophie looks so unhappy.)

Catie glanced at Sophie. "Perhaps she *can't* smile."

"*Everyone* can smile," I argued.

"But Sophie's smile is upside down," Catie sighed.

"Not for long," I promised.

(Pippa Morgan never gives up.)

While Mr Bacon was showing us how to do long division in our next lesson, I passed Sophie a note across the table. It said, *A carrot.* (I knew she'd be dying to know the rest of my parrot joke.)

She read it and stared at me, confused, so I quickly wrote another note to remind her. *What's orange and sounds like a parrot?*

She read it and still looked confused. I guess parrot jokes don't work if you tell them backwards.

So I tried a new joke.

I wrote: *What do you call a three-legged donkey?* I passed Sophie the note and she read it, then I scribbled the answer and flicked it across the table.

That was when the trouble started.

Mr Bacon saw the note and glared at me. "Pippa!" He looked cross. "Why are you and Sophie passing notes?"

"Sophie's not passing notes," I told him quickly. "Just me." How could I explain that I was trying to make her smile? Only Catie was supposed to know about my secret mission.

But Mr Bacon kept frowning. (I think long division makes him cross, which isn't surprising. Long division is horrible.)

"Sophie!" She turned pink as he called out her name. "Read out Pippa's note so everyone can hear it."

In a wobbly voice, Sophie read it out loud. "A wonkey."

Mr Bacon looked confused. So I explained. "It's a joke."

"Not a very funny one." Mr Bacon frowned.

He was totally wrong. "It's funny if you hear the first part!" I grabbed the other note from Sophie's side of the desk but Mr Bacon interrupted before I got a chance to read it.

"Please stop bothering Sophie with jokes and concentrate on maths." Then he threw the piece of paper in the bin. I felt terrible. I hadn't been trying to *bother* Sophie. I just wanted to make her smile. But I'd embarrassed her. And now I couldn't tell her any more jokes.

After maths, Mr Bacon gave us each a list of what we'd be doing on the Isle of Wight. "We're visiting Seaview World on Friday afternoon," he explained as he gave me my list.

He gave a list to Julie. "On Saturday, we're visiting Carisbrooke Castle."

Then Julie threw up on his shoes.

While I watched Julie barf, I thought two things at the same time:

Poor Julie!

Is this a ghostly omen?!

It could be the spirit world sending a warning. Why *else* would the words "Carisbrooke Castle" make someone sick?

Mr Bacon sent Julie straight to the office so the school secretary could look after her and phone her mum. While he was rinsing his shoes, Jenny told us that Julie had woken up feeling poorly but she insisted on coming to school so she didn't miss any pre-trip gossip.

Julie looked really pale as she left the classroom. She *has* to feel better tomorrow. She can't miss the trip. That would be even worse than throwing up on Mr Bacon's shoes.

Here's the list of places we're going to visit:

1. Seaview World Wildlife Park

I wonder if animals have ghosts? If
they do, I might detect hundreds!
Imagine an elephant ghost! Or a tiger
ghost!

2. Carisbrooke Castle

Yep – a real-life castle! Whoop! Whoop!
Mr Bacon says King Charles was held

prisoner there by the Roundheads before they chopped his head off. He didn't explain why the Roundheads chopped his head off. Perhaps the king was a Squarehead?

ANYWAY.

According to Marcus Flaunch, ghosts mostly appear in places where there's been violence or sadness. I bet being a prisoner must be really sad, especially if you're about to have your head chopped off. I bet the king's ghost visits *a lot.*

3. The Ultimate 4D Cinema Experience

I won't be able to hunt ghosts in a 4D
cinema. It's too new to be haunted. I bet
it'll be *ages* before someone
chokes on their popcorn or
dies of fright during a film.

Mum must have finished
cooking. The wok has stopped making
sizzling noises. And the smoke's starting
to clear. Dinner time!

GHOSTS DETECTED: 0 (GHOST OMENS: 1)
SMILE METER: ☹

Friday, 7 a.m.

I have been dressed in my jeans and
Tiffany J hoodie for, like, an hour. I'm
waiting for Dad to fetch me. He's taking
me to the coach at school. It leaves at
eight a.m. Mum's wandering
around like a zombie downstairs.
In her nightie, with her hair all
fuzzy from sleep and
no make-up, she looks
a bit like a ghost. When
I went to get some toast, she
dropped the coffee jar on the
kitchen floor. It sort of exploded
and there were coffee granules
everywhere. They made a really

satisfying crunching noise
when I walked on them.

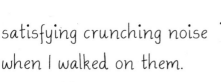

Mum told me to eat my toast in my room
while she cleared them up.

I've texted Dad four times to make sure
he hasn't overslept. His flat is only a
mile away so it won't take long for him
to get here, but when I stay at his place,
he likes to sleep late. Even on *Saturdays*.
Sometimes I think he doesn't realize that
Saturday is the best day of the whole week.
Who wants to sleep through it? I always
make sure I wake him up really early so
he doesn't miss any of it. I hope he's not
sleeping late today.

My phone's buzzing! Squeeeee! That must be him replying.

YAY! He's awake. But his spelling is still sleepy: **AWKE. ON MT WAY. BE THER 15 MNS.** He really needs to use autocorrect more.

I am so excited. Sitting still is really hard. I've checked my bag four times. I've definitely remembered the midnight-feast sweets and my ghost-hunting equipment. This is going to be my first overnight school trip. We are going to have SO MUCH fun! And I'm going to find a ghost. I just

know it. Can't write any more. Too excited. Going to watch out of the window for Dad. . .

On the coach

DISASTER! Julie's <u>still</u> sick and SHE CAN'T COME ON THE TRIP!!!!

Jenny texted Catie this morning and Catie texted me.

I can't believe it. Poor Julie. It must be the worst thing that's ever happened to her! (Apart from throwing up on Mr B's shoes.)

Me and Catie and Jenny have promised to take pictures of *everything* so we can show her when we get back. We could do a presentation, like we're scientists explaining the solar system, with maps

and diagrams and explanations and
everything so she doesn't feel like she's
missed anything.

We were first on the coach and we
took pictures of our seats so Julie could

see them. I sat next to Catie and took
a picture of her, but Mr Bacon came
and said (in his quiet voice like it was
a secret), "Pippa, would you mind sitting
with Sophie? It might be nice for her to
make a new friend. I want her to feel that
our school is welcoming, and if anyone can
make her feel welcome, Pippa, it's you."

That was SO SWEET!

AND it meant I finally had a chance to
talk to Sophie! I could put my Make Sophie
Smile plan into action properly. I wondered
if I should try out the other jokes I'd
learned. Then I decided NO. Last time I
tried, it didn't work out very well. (Oh no!
What if I've put Sophie off jokes FOR EVER?
What will she do at Christmas? Crackers

will never be the same!)

Catie moved to the seat behind me, next to Jenny, which was great because Jenny was feeling lonely without Julie. I think she's worried about not having Julie with her. Jenny and Julie do everything together because they're twins.

The only things they *don't* do together are:

1. Judo.

2. Clarinet.

3. School projects. (Mr Bacon makes them have different project partners.)

4. Eat carrots. (Julie hates carrots
    and Jenny loves carrots. On days
    when they wear the same outfit, the
    only way to tell them apart is to say
    "carrots" and see which one smiles
    and which one pulls an icky face.)

I kept the space next to me free while the
rest of the class filed past and found their
seats. Then I spotted Sophie. She got on
the coach last and looked super-sad. So I
waved at her and called to her to sit next
to me. She just shrugged and squeezed in
beside me with her rucksack.

She's still hugging her rucksack now. I
tried asking her about the trip — I asked

if she was excited and she said no. Then I asked her if she was looking forward to going to Carisbrooke Castle and she said no. So I said she MUST be excited about the 4D cinema and she said no. So I tried asking her about non-trip-related things.

Other things Sophie said no to:

- Do you have any hobbies?

- Do you have any brothers and sisters?

- Do you have a favourite TV programme?

- Do you like pizza?

SHE DOESN'T LIKE PIZZA! I didn't
dare ask her about chicken nuggets.
If she'd said no to chicken nuggets,
my heart might have broken.

So I decided to stop asking her
questions and told her about my pink pig
pyjamas instead, but she just mumbled
and kept looking at the seat in front.

Poor Sophie! She's on the world's most
exciting trip and she's sad.

I've decided to stop bugging her so I can
write my diary. Writing might help me
come up with a new plan.

Everyone else is fizzing with excitement.
Jason and Tom are playing catch at the
back with Darren's rucksack and Mandy

Harrison is talking a hundred miles an hour to Ms Allen, while the rest of the class are chattering to one another. Everyone is smiling, except Sophie. ☹

Yay! Mr Bacon has just told us we can start eating our packed lunches even though it's only nine o'clock. Perhaps eating will cheer Sophie up.

Nope, food doesn't work either. I offered Sophie one of my breakfast crisps. (Having packed lunch for breakfast ROCKS! I want peanut butter sandwiches and crisps *every* morning now.) But Sophie said no. She said she doesn't like salt and

vinegar. I can't imagine
not liking salt and
vinegar. It must be
awful. What does she

put on fish and chips? Dad sometimes
has ketchup on *his* chips, but that's AS
WELL AS salt and vinegar.

Poor Catie had *sushi* for her breakfast.
I nearly died of shock when I leaned over
the back of my seat and watched her open
her ~~lunch~~ breakfast box. It was full of rice
swirls and little fishy
lumps with cucumber
on top. I offered her one
of my sandwiches, but
she said she *liked* sushi. Which is totally
weird after I've introduced her to *chicken*

nuggets. She <u>still</u> doesn't understand good food. Perhaps if she tries one of Dad's pizza face dinners (we make pizzas with topping faces — pepperoni for eyes, pepper slices for hair, sweetcorn for freckles . . . etc.) she'll finally realize that you don't HAVE to enjoy stuff like sushi because there are much yummier things to eat.

I checked out Sophie's breakfast too. She had:

Three cheese triangles.

A packet of cheese puffs.

Four cheese crackers.

A lump of cheese.

Perhaps that's why she's so sad? I like cheese, but if I had to eat it all the time, I'd feel pretty *cheesed off*. 🙁 Then I imagined her family, all eating cheese.

SOPHIE'S MUM: Dinner's ready!

SOPHIE: What are we eating?

SOPHIE'S MUM: Macaroni cheese.

SOPHIE'S DAD: Can I have extra cheese on mine?

SOPHIE'S MUM: Of course! And don't forget, there's cheesecake for pudding!

Perhaps Sophie *hates* cheese but her mum and dad make her eat it ALL THE TIME. Like when my mum decided we should eat more turnips. She put turnips in everything: stew, spag bol, curry. She even served them mashed, with sausages.

IT WAS HORRIBLE. I thought I'd turn into a turnip!

Luckily, she got bored of them and we went back to normal food after a week. But the Turnip Days scarred me for life. I still feel queasy

when I see turnips in the supermarket. I think I may have turniphobia.

I just asked Sophie if she likes turnips. She said no. Then she glanced at me out of the corner of her eye like she was sitting next to a crazy person. I guess it might have seemed like an odd question because she didn't know I'd been thinking about turnips. (Imagine how much easier conversations would be if you knew what the other person was thinking. Being a mind reader would be great! Actually. . . NO! Mind reading would be TERRIBLE! I have enough trouble listening to everything I think. Imagine if I had to listen to other people's thoughts too! I'd probably explode. But I wish I could read *cats'* minds. I've always wondered what cats think about.

And dogs. And *otters*. I bet otters have the cutest thoughts. Like, "Shall I float on my back and let my tummy get dry?" or,

"Wow, this fish tastes even better than I expected.") So I asked Catie and Jenny if they liked turnips, just to make it seem normal. They don't like turnips either. (I must remember to tell Mum that NO ONE likes turnips, just in case she goes turnip bonkers again.)

The coach is whizzing along a motorway. Catie and Jenny are making bracelets while I write in my diary. Sophie's playing a game on her phone.

SAD NEWS!

I feel a bit sad because Mr Bacon just told us who we'll be sharing rooms with. I'm sharing with Sophie. Catie's sharing with Jenny. ☹ I was SO looking forward to sharing with Catie. It was going to be like a three-night sleepover.

But I'll have plenty of time to make Sophie smile. When she sees my pink pig pyjamas, she HAS to smile. They are the best.

Mr Bacon promised that our room will be right next door to Catie and Jenny's. That's quite exciting. We can invent a code and tap messages to each other through the wall just like spies.

Pippa's Secret Code

1 tap = hello

2 taps = are you awake?

3 taps = yes

This is harder than I imagined. Me and Catie usually have a lot more to say to each other than "hello", "are you awake" and "yes".

I know! Dad taught me a code ages ago. His granddad used it when he was a prisoner of war in World War II. He was locked up in a big wooden hut with lots of other prisoners and at night they weren't allowed to talk so they used to tap messages to each other on the sides of their bunks, or on the walls if they were in different rooms.

Great-Granddad Morgan's Code Grid

Number of knocks	1	2	3	4	5
1	A	B	C	D	E
2	F	G	H	I	J
3	K	L	M	N	O
4	P	Q	R	S	T
5	U	V	W	X	Y

You read across, then down, to find the right letter. So one knock followed by four knocks is 1 across, then 4 down, which is P.

My name is 1+4, 4+2, 1+4, 1+4, 1+1.

There's no room in the grid for Z, but I guess Z can share the Y box. We'll just have to remember that:

Zou = You

Zellow = Yellow

Zummy = Yummy

Zucky = Yucky

This is going to be brilliant. I will make grids for Catie, Jenny and Sophie RIGHT NOW!

Catie and Jenny were super-excited when I gave them their grid. They couldn't wait to try out our code. They're practising now by tapping on their sandwich boxes. I was hoping Great-Granddad's code would cheer

Sophie up, but she just said thanks when I gave her the grid, then stared at it for a minute, then looked out of the window. Perhaps she thinks it's too hard. It is kind of hard to begin with. I'll explain it to her later when we're off the coach. She'll love it when I show her how easy it is.

She might even smile. That would be perfect! Especially if I found a ghost straight after.

Pippa Morgan

Official ghost and smile hunter

GHOSTS DETECTED: 0

SMILE METER: ☹

Later

The hotel is fab! Our room has a high
ceiling and big old windows and its
own bathroom. This building *has* to
be haunted. It's so *old!* And there are
miles and miles of corridors and stairs
everywhere. If I was a ghost, I'd definitely
want to hang out somewhere like this.
When I wasn't floating along hallways,
scaring guests, I'd hang out in empty
rooms and order room service. I could
float through the walls. And bounce on the
beds without ruffling the sheets. Awesome
sauce!

I have to write this quickly. We're just

dumping our bags in our rooms before we have lunch and head off to Seaview World. Me and Sophie have got bunk beds and when I asked her whether she wanted to have the top bunk, she said, "I don't mind."

Yay! I got the top bunk. I've never slept in a bunk bed before. It'll be like sleeping on top of the world! I've climbed the ladder six times already. Catie came in to see our bunks. She and Jenny are next door and they've only got ordinary beds. I told Catie she *has* to sleep in the one next to the wall so we can use our secret code even after everyone else is asleep.

Imagine if we're sending coded messages and a ghost starts knocking on the wall! It could send us all kinds of messages about what it's like to be dead. Do ghost eat and drink? Can they see other ghosts? There are so many things I want to ask a ghost:

Can you fly?

Can you float through walls?

What do you think about smartphones and TVs and cars and computers?

Can you speak, or just make scary *wooooooooo* noises?

Can you go anywhere in the world? (Imagine flying to India or Japan! Or perhaps they don't fly. Perhaps they just *imagine* where they want to haunt and then go there. Or perhaps they are stuck in the place where they died.)

Ms Allen's calling us. (She's going to be sleeping in a room at the end of our corridor. The boys are all on the floor underneath us with Mr Bacon.) Gotta go eat lunch. Hotel food! I am SO excited. I wonder if it will be like the food on *Mastercook*?

GHOSTS DETECTED: 0
SMILE METER: ☺

After dinner

Hotel food is definitely not like the food on *Mastercook*. For lunch, we had boring tomato soup. And for tea we had lasagne with carrots. It was kinda like school dinners. (I took a picture of the carrots to show Julie so she didn't feel so sad at missing the trip.)

It's bedtime now and I'm tucked up in the top bunk. The floor is miles below. I'm pretending I'm curled up in a hammock in a rainforest and the ceiling above me is a huge canopy of leaves and the sound of the boys whooping in their rooms downstairs is a troupe of orangutans.

Sophie is underneath me. I asked her if
she wanted to see the photos I took at
Seaview World, but she just shrugged
and said she wanted to read her book.
So that's what she's doing. I can hear

her turning the pages every few minutes.
Apart from that she's totally silent. (My
pink pig pyjamas didn't make her smile,
btw. ☹) I can hear Catie and Jenny
giggling next door.

After tea, I dragged Sophie to their room
and we listened to the new Tiffany J
album and invented some new dance steps
(actually, me, Catie and Jenny invented
dance steps. Sophie just watched). But
then Ms Allen came and said it was time
for bed and me and Sophie had to come
back to our room. Its lights out in twenty
minutes, which gives me just enough time
to write about Seaview World.

Seaview World was awesome. When Mr

Bacon said they didn't have dolphins or sharks, I was pretty sad. But then I saw the otters.

OTTERS ARE FAB!

They have a really lovely enclosure with a big pool. There was a mother otter who just floated around on her back with her front paws folded over her chest like she was sunbathing. And baby otters kept climbing on to her belly, then jumping off into the water. And all the time I kept pretending I was an otter mind reader and imagining what they were thinking:

Hey, let's jump off Mum's tum!

Eek! This water is cold!
Let's have a swimming race!

It was brilliant.

But that wasn't the best
bit.

The flamingos were cool.
They can stand on one leg
for hours, which makes them
look like huge bedside lamps!
I tried standing on one leg
too, but I could only keep my
balance for a second.

But that wasn't the best bit either.

The best bit was when me and Catie and

Jenny and Sophie were allowed to go in with the penguins! I have actually been surrounded by penguins! They didn't come really close, but they made a circle around us and squawked like they were playing ring o' roses. I couldn't stop grinning and Jenny kept squeaking with terror every time a penguin moved closer. Catie wanted to touch one, but the zookeeper who was with us said they might bite. Sophie didn't look excited at all, like it's *normal* to stand around with penguins.

Perhaps it *is* normal for her!

Perhaps her house of full of weird animals. Her dad might be a mad professor who collects strange and rare creatures. She might live in a big rambly old house with giraffes in the hallways and zebras in the kitchen and penguins in every bathroom.

Perhaps she's sad because her dad spends more time with his animals than with her. Or she has to share her room with a hippopotamus.

I think that would make *me* sad.

The zookeeper had a bucket of fish and

she started feeding the penguins. The penguins just opened their beaks and swallowed the fish whole. It was amazing. Like watching socks disappear into the hoover. I'm glad I'm not a penguin. Lasagne may be boring, but swallowing a whole fish must be gross.

When we came out of the penguin enclosure, I asked the zookeeper if she'd ever seen a penguin ghost.

Jason and Tom, who were waiting with the others outside, thought my question was really stupid, and Jason laughed so loud that Mr Bacon had to shush him. But I don't think it was a stupid question. If people can become ghosts, why not penguins? Or meerkats? Or flamingos? Or anything! I bet there must be plenty of ghosts at Seaview World.

I wish we could have stayed there all night. I can just imagine it. Me and Catie could have sneaked away from the group and hidden behind the bins near the café. Then, when everyone had gone home, we could have wandered around the enclosures to hunt for animal ghosts. I could have used my phone to record ghostly noises while Catie checked for cold patches of air. We could have crept around the back of the penguin enclosure. We might have seen ghost penguins, huddled around the edge of the pool, all see-through and wispy. A ghost flamingo might have flown over us while ghost meerkats floated through the walls of their enclosure and ghost otters darted everywhere, their cute otter faces all pale and their big otter eyes staring through the dark.

Wow! It would have been really creepy.

Ms Allen is shouting for us to turn the lights out. I'd better put my diary away. I'm so excited I don't know how I'm going to fall asleep!

ZZZZZZZZZZZZZZZZZZZZZZZZZZZZ

It's six a.m. and I'm the first one awake. Sophie is still asleep in the bunk underneath me. I can hear her making little snorey noises.

This hotel is definitely haunted.

After lights out, me and Catie tried our knocking code (btw, it worked really well). Then something <u>totally mysterious</u>

happened! The lights had been out for fifteen minutes and Catie knocked on the wall. She knocked: H-I P-I-P J-E-N I-S A-S-L-E-E-P and I knocked S-O I-S S-O-P-H-I-E and Catie knocked H-A-S S-H-E S-M-I-L-E-D Y-E-T? and I knocked N-O.

Then there was another knocking noise and I thought it was Catie, but I couldn't work out what she was saying so I knocked W-H-A-T? and she knocked W-H-A-T? so I knocked W-A-S T-H-A-T Y-O-U K-N-O-C-K-I-N-G? and Catie knocked N-O.

My heart started jumping around in my chest. Ghosts are always knocking on *Most Spooky*. So I started waving my hands through the air to feel if it had turned cold, but it hadn't.

ME: D-I-D Y-O-U H-E-A-R T-H-A-T?

CATIE: Y-E-S!

ME: W-A-S I-T A G-H-O-S-T?

CATIE: I D-O-N-T K-N-O-W.

Then I stopped knocking and so did Catie. I was listening for more ghost knocking. But I must have fallen asleep because the next thing I knew there was daylight coming through the curtains and my phone said it was six a.m.

I cannot wait until breakfast to tell everyone that me and Catie heard a ghost.

GHOSTS DETECTED: !!!!!!

SMILE METER: ☹

On the coach

No one believed me! I told everyone on my table about hearing the knocking — Jenny, Amanda, Sophie, Freya and Ms Allen. But they thought I must have dreamt it. Catie told them that she heard it too and Catie is a totally reliable witness. If we were on *CopShop*, Mike Hatchett would have believed us because he always knows when someone's telling the truth. So I used the lie detector test Great-Granddad Morgan taught me. I licked my cereal spoon and dangled it from my nose. ☺

I explained to everyone that if I was lying, the spoon would drop off. Then I said, "I heard a ghost" and the spoon DIDN'T DROP OFF. Complete and total proof! But Ms Allen said it was an old hotel and it was probably just the water pipes banging. Apparently that happens in old buildings.

But it didn't sound anything like pipes banging!!

The whole time I was telling my story about the ghosts, Tom and Jason (who were sitting at the next table with Mr Bacon) kept giggling. Catie said they looked like they were plotting something. But I think they were laughing at my ghost story. I don't know why they think ghosts are funny! They are clearly not in tune with the spirit world like I am. I've only been here one night and I've already had my first ghostly encounter!

I'm SO going to see a ghost at Carisbrooke Castle. We're on our way now. Sophie's sitting beside me playing phone games again. Catie and Jenny are looking at the worksheets Mr Bacon gave us. I keep looking out of the window. Any moment, Carisbrooke Castle is going to appear around a corner. King Charles lived there for months. I bet his spirit is trapped in some dank old dungeon that smells like Dad's old socks in the laundry basket. He'll probably be pleased when I discover him. Being a ghost must be lonely.

OMG!!!

What if he hasn't got a head? The Roundheads cut it off! What if I see a headless ghost?? That would be so cool! He might be holding it under his arm. Imagine having to spend for ever carrying your head around. I wonder if ghost heads are heavy? Perhaps I can lend him my rucksack. It would be far easier to carry it in there.

I've charged my phone so I've got plenty of power to record any sightings. And I'm keeping my hands in my pockets to make sure they're super-warm so I can feel spooky cold air really easily. I'm wearing my fluffy blue jumper of course. The fluff is smooth at the moment (I didn't brush my hair this morning to make sure I didn't get any static on it) so it's ready to detect ghostly energy.

I see it!!!! The castle! On a hill in the distance. It's all old and grey and turrety.

I just asked Sophie if she'd help me look for King Charles's ghost but she said she didn't believe in ghosts. So I asked her about the ghost in our room last night, and she just said it was the pipes like Ms Allen said.

Poor Sophie. I have to make her smile soon. Her imagination must be dying. She's starting to think like a grown-up! I just wish it wasn't so hard. I tried at breakfast time. When she left the table to fetch some orange juice, I moved her toast and sausages and eggs into a smiley face on her plate. But when she sat down again, she didn't even notice! She just stabbed the sausage mouth with her fork and dipped it in the egg eye. Poor breakfast face. ☹

Oooh, we're in the castle car park. It's time to put my diary away and start the biggest ghost hunt of my life!

GHOSTS DETECTED: 1

(NO MATTER WHAT MS ALLEN SAYS)

SMILE METER: ☹

On the coach

Carisbrooke Castle was amazing! Catie
and Jenny are sitting behind me playing
with the snow globes they bought at the
gift shop. Sophie's sitting next to me. And
she's actually NOT looking sad!

The castle was really big and it took ages
to walk around. We had a tour guide
who told us that there had been LOTS
of ghost sightings at the castle. There's a
myth that a woman drowned in the well
hundreds of years ago and sometimes
her face appears in the well water. Me and
Catie looked down, but it was so deep we
couldn't see anything except shadows. And

my jumper didn't prickle. But the well did make lots of spooky, echoey noises when we shouted "Are you there, drowned lady?" down it.

Then the guide told us about another myth — the Grey Lady, a ghost with a long cloak and four dogs, is supposed to walk around the castle at night. I wish I was the Grey Lady. It would be so cool to have four dogs to walk — especially if one of them was a labradoodle. I love labradoodles!

I asked if anyone had ever seen King Charles's ghost, but the guide said no.

And I said, "Not yet."

I swear, my jumper started to tingle as I said it.

While we were looking around, Sophie put her hand up and asked if she could go to the loo.

Mr Bacon asked me to go with her so we didn't get lost. So we crossed the courtyard together and went into the hall on the other side. Then we followed the toilet signs along a corridor, and when we found the loos, Sophie went in.

While I was waiting outside, I heard footsteps in the distance. I peered down the corridor, but I couldn't see anyone. But the footsteps got louder. Then the fluff on my blue jumper started prickling along my arms. I pulled my phone out of my pocket, but before I could find the video setting, a man appeared at the end of the corridor.

I froze!

I could hardly believe my eyes. The man had a pointy black beard, and old-fashioned clothes, and a cloak and long curly hair.

I was staring at King Charles!

I was so scared and excited, my mouth turned dry. I wanted to call out to Sophie but all I could do was stand and stare while the ghost of King Charles walked right past me and disappeared around the corner at the other end of the corridor. I felt the wind from his cloak rush over me. It was so cold it made me shiver.

I didn't even notice Sophie come out of the loos. I was too busy staring after the ghost, my heart hammering so hard I could hear it in my ears!

Sophie nudged me, then squeaked as my blue jumper gave her an electric shock.

That brought me back to my senses. I was suddenly unfrozen.

"Quick!" I shouted and grabbed her arm. I raced down the corridor, chasing the ghost. I fumbled with my phone so I could snap a picture, but running and finding phone settings isn't easy, and I was still dragging Sophie after me.

"What is it?" she puffed.

"A ghost!" A door was swinging shut ahead of us as we skidded around the corner. I barged through it in time to see King Charles striding across the courtyard.

I stopped, lifted my camera and took a photo. I just managed to snap him before

he disappeared through another door that said "No Entry" on it.

Sophie stopped and pulled me back. "We can't go in there! We're not allowed."

I stared at her,

my thoughts whizzing a million miles an hour. What would Marcus Flaunch do? He'd NEVER let a No Entry sign stand between him and the ghost of King Charles. He'd barge right through, waving his ghost-detecting machines. "But we *have* to!" I squeaked. "That was the ghost of King Charles!"

Sophie actually blinked. She looked excited!

Then she slid past me and opened the door — carefully, like there might be a tiger waiting on the other side.

We both peeked in.

A narrow corridor stretched ahead, then turned a corner. There was no sign of King Charles.

Just as I was about to creep past Sophie and go inside, a shout sounded behind us. I spun round and saw Mr Bacon waving to us across the courtyard. The rest of the class were huddled around him. "Did you get lost?" he called.

Ms Allen was beside him. "You can't go in there!" she told us. "It says 'No Entry'."

My heart dropped like a stone.

I wanted to see where my ghost had gone. My jumper was fluffed out like a frightened cat's fur.

(I immediately decided to write to Marcus Flaunch to tell him to get a fluffy jumper because they are way better at detecting ghosts than his old equipment.)

"Come on." Sophie tugged me towards the class. They were already heading for a building further along the courtyard.

"Why did you take so long?" Catie whispered as we slid in beside her.

I was about to tell her about the ghost, but then Sophie did something so surprising that I forgot to speak.

Sophie WINKED at me. It was a secret, special wink, like we were real friends. I felt instantly happy.

"I'll tell you later," I whispered to Catie.

I followed the group, fizzing with excitement, and we went to look in the castle keep. There was a donkey wheel beside another well. Apparently, the well is so deep that it needs a donkey to walk round the wheel (it looks like a huge wooden hamster wheel) just to wind the bucket all the way to the top.

That's when Jason started teasing me.

He said really loudly, "Hey, Pippa. Ask the castle guide if there are any donkey ghosts here." And everyone laughed. Then he said that if there were penguin ghosts in Seaview World, and pipe-banging ghosts at the hotel, there *must* be donkey ghosts here.

I knew I had a real ghost picture on my phone and I *had* to prove that I can see ghosts.

So I showed him the photo. "Look. It's the

ghost of King Charles!"

Jason stared at it and for the first time EVER he didn't say anything. He just looked a bit pale.

He hardly said anything all the way to the next building — it was the same building my ghost king had disappeared into. I was REALLY excited. My tummy was doing a *double* fizz. What if we saw him again? What if he appeared in front of the whole class? It would be the best ghost sighting in the world and *prove* that I am a total ghost magnet. Marcus Flaunch would beg me to be on his TV programme...

gasps

. . . I could have my own TV programme!

Millions of people would watch me every week discovering ghosts all over the world!

I nudged Sophie as we went through the door. "Tell me if you see him," I whispered.

"OK," she whispered back.

Catie leaned closer. "What are you whispering about?"

"You'll see in a minute," I told her. I

just knew that King Charles would appear again. As we followed the tour guide into a big room, I checked my jumper, but it had stopped prickling. I wiggled my fingers, feeling for cold patches of air. But the air inside was warm.

I was so busy scanning the room for ghostly presences, I hardly heard the tour guide announce that a member of the castle staff would be giving us a talk.

Then I saw my ghost!

He walked through an archway, stood in front of the class and bowed.

It was really happening! My ghost was appearing in front of the whole class.

The tour guide held out his arm and said, "Here is the king. He's going to tell you what it was like being a prisoner in Carisbrooke Castle in the 1640s."

I blinked. The tour guide was acting like my ghost was the most ordinary thing in the world. Did King Charles appear *every* day?

Then I suddenly realized that my ghost was wearing a wig. And his clothes were a costume. My ghost wasn't a ghost. It was an actor, dressed in a King Charles costume.

I must have seen him hurrying to get ready to give his talk.

I started to feel hot. I could feel my face turning red. I was just about to die of embarrassment when Jason pointed at the actor and laughed. "Look, Pippa. It's your ghost!" Then he laughed even louder and called to the actor. "Pippa thought you were a ghost!"

Everyone started laughing. Even Ms Allen.

If I *had* died of embarrassment, I would have haunted Jason Matlock for the rest of his life.

Then Catie put her arm round me and gave me a quick squeeze. "Never mind, Pippa," she said. "I'm sure you'll find a real ghost soon."

Sophie squished in next to me and whispered, "*I* thought it was a real ghost too." And she gave me a sympathetic smile.

Suddenly I felt better.

OK, it wasn't a *happy* smile, but it *was* a smile. Perhaps I haven't found my ghost yet, but at least I've started to cheer Sophie up.

We had a packed lunch in the castle grounds after that. Me and Catie shared a picnic bench with Sophie and Jenny. Sophie and Jenny swapped sandwiches

(Sophie likes cheese after all), and I offered to swap my plain crisps for Sophie's salt and vinegar ones. She looked really pleased.

When we got back on the coach, Sophie sat next to me like she really wanted to instead of because she had to. And when I suggested a game of I Spy, she said yes.

I spied something beginning with C. Sophie guessed a gazillion things. Car. Cow. Cloud. Coat. But she was looking out of the coach window. I was looking at the crocodile plushie dangling from Mandy Harrison's rucksack. When Sophie finally followed my gaze and saw it, she squeaked

"Crocodile" so loudly that she blushed and put her hands over her mouth as though she'd just accidentally burped.

It almost felt like we were proper friends. So I asked her about her old school. I wanted to find out if she used to go to a girls' school (Reasons Sophie Might Be Sad #2) but she said no. It was a school just like ours. Then she started to look miserable again, so I quickly told her it was her turn at I Spy and she started looking for something to spy.

I started crossing things off the list in my head.

Reasons Sophie Might Be Sad

- ~~Extra toe~~

- ~~Too much cheese~~

- ~~Having to go to school with boys~~

Then Sophie interrupted my thinking by saying really quickly, "I-spy-with-my-little-eye-something-beginning-with-T." She was looking out of the window, so I looked too. The coach was whizzing past a red phone box. I shouted "Telephone box" and I was right! First guess! The box looked *really* old, like the ones on the TV programmes Mum likes to watch.

I wonder if Marcus Flaunch has ever investigated a haunted phone box? I can imagine watching *Most Spooky* with Marcus and Sally Pippin squished into a phone box, while Marcus is having one of his psychic moments.

MARCUS: Can you feel the cold?

SALLY: (huddled beside him) I'm actually feeling rather warm.

MARCUS: There's definitely a presence in here. My energy meter is off the scale.

Then the phone suddenly rings.

Sally screams.

Marcus answers it and a ghostly voice says, "The *last* person I phoned never escaped from here. . ."

That would be SO scary!

Perhaps it's good that King Charles didn't turn out to be a real ghost. He's probably still quite cross about having his head chopped off by Roundheads. Kings don't expect to get their heads chopped off. They're usually the ones who do the chopping. If he *had* been real and spotted me chasing him with my phone, he might have thought I was a Roundhead and started chasing me!!

The sun's come out so I've taken off my ghost-hunting blue jumper. I think I need a break from ghost hunting. I wonder what the cinema will be like?

GHOSTS DETECTED: 0
SMILE METER: ☺

At the hotel after tea

Dinner was great. I am SO full! We had three courses. It was like having three separate dinners. First we had minestrone soup with alphabet pasta in it. Catie wrote CATIE, SOPHIE and JENNY on the edge of her bowl. Then Jenny rearranged the letters and spelled I ENJOY NICE PEAS.

I wrote GHOSTS with my pasta.

The soup was quite cold when we finally ate it, but it still tasted nice.

Then we had something chickeny. It was much nicer than the lasagne (but not as good as nuggets). Pudding was even better.

It was chocolate sponge but all runny
in the middle. It was so delicious Jason
asked for seconds. But the waiter said they
didn't serve second helpings in hotels and
gave him a look like he'd rather be feeding
penguins. So Jason licked his plate. Then
Tom licked his plate, and before long all the
boys were licking their plates. I wanted to
lick my plate but I didn't want to end up
with a chocolate nose like Jason's. So I just
used my spoon to scrape up all the sauce.

We're back in our rooms now. I'm lying
on my bunk like a big washed-up whale. I
may have to go running through the hotel
corridors after I've had a good burp. I need
to work up an appetite. It's our midnight

feast in two and a half hours. HURRAH!

But first I have to write about what happened at the 4D cinema!

It was a film about being under the sea. We were all wearing 3D glasses (I love sitting in a room where everyone's wearing the same glasses. It looks so weird, like a robot festival). My seat kept jiggling about and pummelling me when something on-screen was moving or getting pummelled. And when there was wind in the film, real wind blasted over me. And water sprayed everyone. It was brilliant. Then there were bubbles rising around us like we were underwater. At first there were just a few bubbles. But then there were more and more until I couldn't see the screen any more. Bubbles were *everywhere*. One of the cinema staff raced down the steps to the front and started fiddling with a machine under the screen. The ushers opened the exit doors and waved their arms around, trying to flap the bubbles out of the cinema.

A whisper rippled along our row until Catie murmured in my ear: "The bubble machine's broken."

Mr Bacon and Ms Allen got up and started trying to flap the bubbles away.

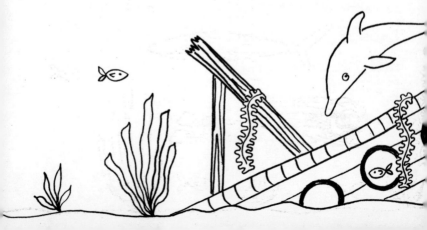

Then everyone was standing up, flapping,
and bubbles were swirling everywhere.
No one was watching the film any more.
I helicoptered my arms but it just made
the bubbles swirl around me even more.
It was like being an underwater explorer,
except I could breathe. I started to imagine
swimming past dolphins and sharks
and finding a wrecked ship lying at the
bottom of the ocean. I flapped my arms
harder and pretended I was swimming
through the portholes and up and down
the seaweed-covered
decks.

We didn't need the movie at all. I glanced at Sophie next to me. She was splatting bubbles between her hands. I'm sure she was smiling but it was hard to tell through all the flapping and bubbles.

Sophie has just climbed up to my bunk.

SOPHIE: *(looking at my pink pig pyjamas)* I like your pyjamas.

ME: *(grinning proudly and scooting over to make room for her)* Thanks.

SOPHIE: *(pointing at my diary)* What are you doing?

ME: Writing in my ghost-hunting journal.

SOPHIE: That's so cool! (*making herself comfortable at the end of my bunk*) Do you like jelly babies?

ME: I love them.

SOPHIE: Good, because I've got some for the midnight feast.

GHOSTS DETECTED: 0
SMILE METER: ☺

After midnight

This the latest I've ever stayed up (except for the New Year's Eve when Uncle Pete climbed on to the roof to celebrate and got stuck and Mum had to call the fire brigade).

It's been the best night ever (even better than New Year's Eve). We're going home tomorrow but I will remember tonight for ever and ever.

We waited until after lights out, then I knocked on Catie's wall.

ME: C-O-M-E T-O O-U-R R-O-O-M.

CATIE: O-K.

Then I heard someone else knocking on the wall below me. At first I thought it was the ghostly knocking from last night. Then I realized it was using our code.

G-O-T J-E-L-L-Y B-A-B-I-E-S.

I dangled my head over the side of my bunk and saw that Sophie was sitting with her phone shining on to her code grid and knocking a message through the wall.

I grinned at her and hopped down out of my bunk, landing as quietly as possible. I didn't want Ms Allen to come to check on us.

Then there was a soft tap on the door and I let Catie and Jenny in.

They'd brought their duvets with them and we pulled all the sheets off our beds and made a fantastic sheet fort using the chairs from the other side of the room. Then we dragged our duvets and pillows inside. It was SO comfy. Jenny had brought a torch and we used it as a lamp and we all emptied our sweets stash into a pile in the middle.

Then we snuggled under our duvets and started eating.

Catie had brought liquorice wands and cinder toffee (that yummy puffy honeycomb stuff that sticks in your teeth) and Jenny had brought chocolate

melts and fizz bombs and I'd brought
gummy snakes and a whole box of
white chocolate cats, which Uncle
Pete had given me for my birthday. Sophie
had brought two whole bags of jelly babies
and some peppermint toffees. She also had
a huge bag of cheese puffs.

"I love cheese," she said as she opened
them.

That gave me a brilliant idea. Jelly baby
and cheese puff sandwiches! I squashed a
jelly baby between two puffs and ate it in
one mouthful. It was really quite nice. The
salty puffs and the sweet jelly gummed
into my teeth and it tasted really nice
when I sucked it out again.

I made Catie try one and she quite liked

it but Jenny said, "No way." Sophie said she liked cheesy puffs so much she didn't want to ruin the taste with jelly babies.

Then Catie ate a peppermint toffee and a fizz bomb at the same time. She looked so happy as she chewed it that we all tried. Peppermint-toffee fizz bombs are fabulous.

I was just about to try a cinder-toffee-chocolate-melt combo when I heard The Knocking.

ME: (freezing like a surprised mouse) Shh!!!!

CATIE: (with her mouth still full of toffee bomb) Wha'?

JENNY: (*stretching a gummy snake*) I didn't hear anything.

SOPHIE: (*putting her finger on her lips*) Shhh!!!

We all went quiet and listened.
The Knocking came again.

Catie's eyes grew round as headlights. "Who can be knocking??? There's  no one next door! We're all here!"

JENNY: (*winding the gummy snake around her finger*) It's probably just the pipes, like Ms Allen said.

ME: Does that sound like pipes to you? (The knocking was quite soft, like Catie's code knocks but more thuddy.) Pipes don't go thud, they go clang.

SOPHIE: (*leaning down and listening hard*) It's coming through the floor.

Catie gasped and wriggled deeper under her duvet. Jenny started chewing on her gummy snake.

Sophie flipped on to her belly and pressed her ear to the floor.

The knocking started again.

Thud thud thud thud.

"It's underneath us," Sophie said.

The thudding went on.

Catie squeaked. "It's a ghost. I know it's a ghost!"

"There's no such thing as ghosts," Jenny said.

Thud thud thud.

"Yes, there are!" I told her. My heart was beating really fast now. I was half scared and half excited. This could be my chance to find a ghost — a real ghost — to put in my ghost-hunting journal! I squirmed from under my duvet and fought my way out of the fort. The air outside was freezing cold. That was a definite sign of a ghostly presence.

Thud thud thud.

I grabbed my blue fluffy jumper from under the bunks and put it on. It crackled with static and I'm sure my hair must have been standing on end as it fizzed right through me. The thudding was getting louder. I stuck my head back into the fort. "This is the scariest and best thing ever!" Sophie was still listening through the floor. Catie was peeping over the top of her duvet. Jenny was gathering

128

up our sweets stash in a pillowcase.

Then the thudding stopped.

Catie froze and stared at me. "Has the ghost gone?"

Sophie sat up. "It's either gone, or it's coming to get us."

"No!" Catie squeaked and disappeared beneath her duvet.

"Don't worry! I know what to do." Tbh, I hadn't got a clue what to do. What if the ghost WAS coming to get us? My ghost-hunting journal would end with empty pages. I would end up covered in spooky slime.

The ghost might steal our sweets!

I pushed away my scary thoughts and ducked out of the fort.

Then I heard footsteps.

Loud, slow footsteps in the hallway outside. And they were heading towards our door.

"It's coming!" Jenny scrambled out of the fort. Sophie followed. Catie poked her head out between the sheets. The torch glowed spookily on her face as it rolled across the floor.

The footsteps stopped.

Then something banged

on our door three times. We all squealed.

I signalled for the others to stay back. After all, I was the most experienced ghost hunter. I'd watched *Most Spooky*. And I'd got a ghost book out of the library. I tried to imagine what Marcus Flaunch would do.

The banging sounded again.

Marcus would try to speak with The Presence.

I crept towards the door. "Who's there?" My voice was trembling.

A low wail sounded beyond the door.

A second voice began moaning. Then it broke into a spooky cackle.

The wailing voice started to cackle too, a crazy cackle that made the hair on my neck stand on end.

"There are two of them!" Catie sobbed. She was outside the fort, clinging on to Jenny.

Sophie was staring at the door through narrowed eyes, like she was planning something.

The spooky cackling died away.

I was breathing so fast I could hardly speak. But I imagined I *was* Marcus Flaunch. *They want to communicate,* I told myself. *They must have something important to tell me.* Suddenly I felt special. Out of all the hotel guests, these ghosts had chosen *me.* I straightened my shoulders. I was going to help these poor lost souls find the peace they needed.

"Speak to me," I called through the door, feeling exactly like Marcus Flaunch. Then I tried out one of his lines. "Let me guide you to your final rest."

"Piiiiiiipppppppppppaaaaaaaa." One of the ghosts was calling my name!

My heart felt like it was going to burst. My fluffy jumper was prickling like I was being rubbed with balloons. And the draught from under the door was so icy my feet felt like I was standing in snow. I pressed the record button on my phone.

"What do you want?" I asked, quoting Marcus Flaunch. Part of me wanted to run and hide in the fort and scream till Ms Allen came to rescue us. But I had to find out what these ghosts wanted.

There was another spooky cackle – well, actually, it sounded more like a giggle now – then a voice came through the door. "We want youuuuuuuuuuuu!"

I backed away. I was shaking now. This *never* happened to Marcus Flaunch. If it did, I bet Sally Pippin would have fainted and Marcus would have dropped his recording equipment and run away.

"Help!" Catie sounded hysterical with fear. She climbed into the top bunk. Jenny clambered after her and they hugged each other, their eyes wild with terror.

Sophie hadn't moved. She was staring at the door, looking thoughtful.

I blinked at her. "Aren't you scared?"

"No." She turned and headed for the bathroom. A moment later, she came back carrying two big white towels. She marched towards the door, flinging one of the towels towards me. I caught it and stared at her. "What's this for?"

"Listen," she whispered and pressed her head against the door.

I leaned my head beside hers and heard sniggering on the other side.

"It's Jason and Tom," Sophie whispered. "They were making the knocking noise too. I bet their room is under ours. They were thumping on their ceiling."

I pressed my ear harder against the wood. The spluttery giggles did sound more like boys than ghosts. I didn't know whether to feel relieved or disappointed.

Then Sophie put her towel over her head.

"Copy me," she breathed.

I flung the towel over my head. "What are we doing?" Was this Sophie's idea of hiding?

"We're being ghosts!" she told me. "Sound scary!" She turned the handle and flung open the door. "Woooooooooooooooooo!"

I lifted my arms, making the towel flap, and gave a blood-curdling shriek.

"Waaaaaaaaaaaaaaaaaaaaaa!"

Two terrified screams exploded in front of us. Footsteps thudded over carpet. I pulled the towel from my head in time to see Jason and Tom racing down the corridor, wails of terror trailing behind them.

Behind me, Catie whimpered. She'd climbed down from my bunk. Jenny was peering over her shoulder. "What was it?"

"Jason and Tom," I told her. "They were pretending to be ghosts."

Sophie pulled the towel from her head. She was grinning. A big wide smile that pushed her cheeks up and wrinkled her eyes. She looked so happy!

"I think *our* ghosts were more convincing."

"We were definitely more scary." I grinned back at her. "How did you guess it was Jason and Tom?"

Sophie flung the towel over her shoulder and headed back to the fort. "I recognized Jason's annoying giggle."

Ms Allen knocked on the door a few moments later and asked if everything was OK. We told her about Jason and Tom and how we'd scared them more than they'd scared us. She wasn't cross. Even though I saw her peeking over her shoulder towards our fort. She just said, "Well, I'm glad you're all OK." She glanced at Sophie, who was still smiling, and grinned. "Have fun." Then she went back to her room.

So we got to finish our midnight feast, and once we'd got over the sugar rush and started to feel tired, Catie and Jenny went back to their room while me and Sophie brushed our teeth.

When we were lying in our bunks, I told Sophie that today had been one of my best days since I starred in the school talent show with Catie.

SOPHIE: Talent show?

ME: Yep. We danced and we came second. It was great.

SOPHIE: (thoughtfully) Is Catie your best friend?

ME: Yes.

SOPHIE: Have you been friends for ever?

ME: We hardly knew each other last year. Rachel was my best friend then.

SOPHIE: What happened to Rachel?

ME: She moved to Scotland.

SOPHIE: Do you miss her?

ME: Yes, but not as much as I used to. I made friends with Catie, and although I miss having Rachel around, I'm really happy to have Catie and

Jenny and Julie.

Sophie went quiet for a bit, then she
said in a sad voice, "I miss my friends."

"From your old school?" I asked.

"Yes." There was a crack in her voice like
she wanted to cry.

That's when I realized. Sophie
wasn't sad because she had an extra
toe or her family were cheese
freaks or there was a hippo in
her bedroom. She was sad
because she was missing
her friends.

I hung my head over the edge
of the bunk to check she was OK. She
looked at me with big eyes.

ME: I know how you feel, but you'll feel better soon, I promise. Especially now you have new friends.

SOPHIE: (*blinking at me*) *New* friends?

ME: Catie, Jenny and me, of course!

I gave her my biggest grin and she grinned back.

SOPHIE: Thanks, Pippa.

ME: Thanks, Sophie.

SOPHIE: What for?

ME: Making this one of the best weekends ever.

Sophie grinned again. It was as if all the smiles she'd kept inside since she moved here were finally bursting out. She rolled over and went to sleep after that, which gave me the chance to write my ~~diary~~ ghost-hunting journal.

I can't stop smiling either. So what if I didn't find a real ghost in the Isle of Wight? I can always watch Marcus Flaunch find ghosts on *Most Spooky*. The most important thing is, I managed to make Sophie smile. And now she's my friend.

And making a new friend is better than seeing a hundred ghosts.

GHOSTS DETECTED: 0 (so far)
SMILE METER: 😁

P.S. I *still* might see a hundred ghosts. Mum says we're going to Wales this summer and there are loads of castles there. If we visit them all, I *know* I'll definitely see a ghost!

THE PROS AND CONS OF HAVING A GHOST PET

PROS

#1: Space wouldn't be an issue so you could have whatever animal you liked as a pet — like a gorilla or an elephant or even a whale! Who wouldn't want a whale as a pet?!

#2: You wouldn't ever have to feed them, so all the money you would have spent on pet food could be spent on something way more fun — like taking them to the circus or bungee jumping.

#3: You wouldn't have to clean up their

poo!! Unless ghost pets do ghost poos...?
I'll have to look it up on Wikipedia.

#4: You'd never have to take them
to the vet because they'd never get
poorly.

#5: They would NEVER DIE because they're
already dead!

<u>CONS</u>

#1: Ghost pets aren't cuddly so you can't
snuggle up to them or stroke them. If you
tried to stroke them, your hand would
probably go right through them, which is
kind of gross.☹

#2: They might not poo or wee but they would leave slime everywhere. (Jason says he watched a movie about ghosts and they left green slime all over the house they were haunting.) I think I'd prefer being a pooper-scooper than a slime-scraper.

#3: Your friends wouldn't be able to see them – unless they were able to see ghosts too but not many people are able to see ghosts so that's unlikely. And if they couldn't see your pet they might think you were just pretending and then you'd be

known in school as *The Girl With The Imaginary Pet*, which would be really embarrassing.

#4: It would be really cold all the time with a ghost pet around — even in summer. I suppose I could wear lots of jumpers and scarves but having to get changed every time I left them would be pretty annoying.

#5: They could escape at any time because they'd be able to float through the bars of the cage. And the walls of the house!!! That would be SO STRESSFUL!

PIPPA MORGAN'S
TOP TEN GHOST JOKES

How do ghosts like their eggs cooked?
Terror-fried

What do ghosts eat for dinner?
Spook-ghetti

What do ghosts like for dessert?
Ice-scream

What's a ghost's favourite fairground ride?
The roller-ghoster

How do ghosts travel to another country?
By scare-plane

When do ghosts play tricks on each other?
April Ghouls' Day

Which ghost ate too much porridge?
Ghouldilocks

What do you call a dinosaur ghost?
A terror-dactyl

Where do ghosts mail their letters?
At the ghost office

What's a ghost's favourite game?
Hide and shriek

PIPPA MORGAN'S
TOP-SECRET CODE FOR BFFs

Great-Granddad's code is great, but what if there aren't any walls to knock on?

DISASTER!

That's why I've invented a SUPER-secret code for me and my best friends to use. You just need a piece of paper. Oh, and you also have to know the alphabet.

Here's what you do. You move every letter in the alphabet along one place, so a becomes b, b becomes c, c becomes d, and so on... Simples!

NZ OBNF JT QJQQB NPSHBO

MY NAME IS PIPPA MORGAN

DIJDLFO OVHHFUT BSF UIF CFTU

CHICKEN NUGGETS ARE THE BEST

UJGGBOZ K SPDLT

TIFFANY J ROCKS

How cool is that?! Not even Mr Bacon will
be able to crack it...